THE SECRET DRAWER CLUB

BARBE TURNER
with a foreword by Eddie Coker

illustrations by
~ Andrew Q. Holzschuh! ~

BROWN BOOKS KIDS

The Secret Drawer Club

Brown Books Kids
16250 Knoll Trail Drive, Suite 205
Dallas, Texas 75248
www.BrownBooksKids.com
(972) 381-0009

A New Era in Publishing™

ISBN 978-1-61254-175-4
LCCN 2014943272

Printed in the United States
10 9 8 7 6 5 4 3 2 1

For more information or to contact the author, please go to www.Wezmore.com

Written with TLC for Honey's Love Bugs:
Savannah, McAmis & Caleb

CONTENTS

FOREWORD

As a singer/songwriter and performer who has had the joy of entertaining over a million children in live concert venues across this great country, a long-time mission of mine has been to trumpet the message: Be you. You. Not him, not her, not anyone but the one and only you. So I am going to be me.

I love how Barbe Turner writes. Huge big love how she writes. I love additionally her wit, her charm, her style, and her panache. And yes, boys and girls, you might have to look that last word up starting with a P in the previous sentence but that's OK because expanding one's vocabulary is great fun! Guess what? Barbe will help develop your vocabulary too!

I can't wait for you to read *The Secret Drawer Club*. My guess is she will reel you in pretty quickly. I was "reeled" one night around 11:00 PM. I go to bed at 9. I didn't want to read at 11. I wanted to be horizontal. It took one sentence and I was awake. *Wide*-awake.

What she shared with me that night was written for a dear friend of hers, a woman named Rosemary. After being blown away by *how* she wrote—that style I was intimating in an aforementioned paragraph—my bedtime was pushed further forward into the night because a conversation ensued.

We began talking about how we struggle as human beings and how deeply people need one another. Whoa. Not only was she good, she was willing to explore the deeper complexities of life on the planet.

Houston. We have lift off!

Thank you, thank you, oh ye things out in the big blue sky who align "stuff" together! Thank you.

While this may be her first children's book ever, it won't be her last. How do I know? I've read the other ones. And one day, my deepest wish is that you will read them too.

With that being said, every journey of a 1000 miles begins with one step. Here's to

Barbe, *The Secret Drawer Club*, and here's to you, the human being who is letting me be me. Boom. Let's go.

Eddie Coker

Manitou Springs, Colorado

May 2014

AUTHOR'S NOTE

I owe the birth of *The Secret Drawer Club* and "Barbe the children's author" to a happy circumstance of renewed acquaintance with a classmate from my high school days. You all will know him as Eddie Coker, renowned children's entertainer. I am fortunate enough to know him as friend. When Eddie asked me if I would consider taking the charming characters from the lyrics of his songs and bring them to life in book form, I was at once honored and horror-stricken. I have been writing all my life, but aside from articles in religious/motivational publications in my early years, my writing has been limited to stories for personal and family enjoyment only. I had little to no confidence in my ability to write a book for children. But with Eddie's belief and passion and the encouragement of my family, I decided to give it a go. Eddie provided me with lyrics to several of his captivating songs. Songs of Happy Ones, a hippopotamus opera star, and philanthropic grasshoppers ran rampant in my imagination, creating stories that I pray will one day grace the bookshelves of young readers. But the song of "Maralissa Lou" was the one that haunted me day and night, just begging to be told in story form. My question was this: "Just how do I go about telling it?" One day, Eddie shared with me an experience of a young friend of his. This young woman told of a secret drawer that existed in her high school. Upon discovery of this drawer, she opened it to find a note of encouragement left behind by the last person to discover the drawer—an inspiration to the next who opened it. Thus was the chain of the secret drawer kept alive by many a love-giving soul in her school. I cherished this idea so much that it began to mingle with my love for "Maralissa Lou," until suddenly *The Secret Drawer Club* became so much a reality that it flowed straight from some outward source much greater than I right onto the paper in front of me. I hope you enjoy reading *The Secret Drawer Club* as much as I enjoyed having it flow through me.

ACKNOWLEDGMENTS

Thank you to the following individuals who, without their contributions and support, this book would not have been written:

To my greatest fans, toughest critics, and best friends—Lucy Rose, Mitchell, and McCary—I thank you for your constant and unswerving devotion and confidence in your Mama.

To my fan club from above—Rosemary and Mom—I thank you for being my perfect, loving, and supportive role models and guardian angels. You are a tough act to follow.

To my indispensable loves from the home front—John, Daphne, Sunshine, and Mimi—I thank you for the hugs and sloppy kisses that keep me in love with life on a daily basis.

To my unwitting muse—Erica—I thank you for your story of your very own Secret Drawer Club.

To my partner in crime—Eddie Coker—I thank you not only for "Maralissa Lou," but also for believing in me, oftentimes, for me.

To my publisher—Milli Brown, and the supportive group of professionals at Brown Books Publishing Group—I thank you for doing what you do best.

MARALISSA LOU
By Eddie Coker

His name was Maralissa Lou.
Yes, I know; I thought the same thing too.
What kind of name is that?

I was walking home one day when he
stopped me on the street and said,
"Can we talk for a while?"

And he said,
"Now I know my ears are kind of big,
and my hair's a wee bit strange.
But that's the way that I was made.
I don't think that I can change.

I really have a mom and dad like you
who have loved me from the start,
And though my face is truly polka-dot,
I have a human heart."

I did not know quite what to say
as I lowered my head and walked away.
How could I be so mean?
We used to laugh and run away,
Find a place to hide so he would say,
"Hey, why won't you play with me?"

"Now I know his ears are kind of big
and his hair's a wee bit strange.
But that's the way that he was made,
I don't think that he can change.

He really has a mom and dad like me
who have loved him from the start.
And though his face is truly polka-dot,
he has a human heart."
And his heart gets glad.
And his heart gets mad.
And his heart gets sad like everybody else.

He's just like me.
He's just like you.
A polka-dotted little boy
whose name is Maralissa Lou.

ZIM

Zack "Zim" Zimmerman was ten the year of the Secret Drawer Club. He was almost five feet tall by then, a good foot taller than most boys in his class. He was athletic and exceptionally good looking, with wavy, red hair; long, curly eyelashes;

and dimples that looked like little crescent moons carved into his rosy cheeks. His smile managed to get him out of all kinds of trouble, and it didn't hurt that his sky-blue eyes literally sparkled when he was interested in the topic of conversation, which was pretty much always. On top of all of that, he had a really good heart. So it wasn't surprising to hear he was extremely popular among the other fifth graders at William E. Zane Elementary, even though he'd only lived in the neighborhood since the summer.

Zim and his family—which consisted of his mom, Julie; his dad, Bruce; his three-year-old sister, Savannah; and a cranky, orange marmalade cat named Mr.

Jam Jams—moved to the little midwestern town of Zanesville in the beginning of June.

Zim was used to moving often, since his dad's job with Celestial Hotels and Resorts was to open, manage, and train the staff of small boutique hotels. The new hotel in Zanesville, The Celestial Pearl, was to host forty-nine luxury suites overlooking beautiful Lake Pearl, from which the new hotel took its name. From start to finish, the projects usually took about two years to accomplish. As soon as the hotels were running up to Bruce Zimmerman's high standards, he and his family would move on to the next town in need of a swanky new hotel. Consequently, Zim had learned to adapt quickly to his new surroundings and to make friends rather easily.

He met Sophie, Grace, Jake, and Noah at Ebenezer Park and Pool, named for the *E* in William E. Zane, the day after the Zimmermans moved into the white two-story house with the wraparound porch on Red Wolf Lane. Julie Zimmerman, who had her hands full trying to keep little Savannah occupied while simultaneously unpacking the pictures and knickknacks that turned each new house into a home, shooed Zim out the door after a breakfast of scrambled cheesy eggs, link sausage, and a tall glass of pulp-free orange juice. She gave him a kiss on the head and instructions to go make new friends and have a good time.

Which is exactly what he did. He walked right up to the foursome as they were about to launch into a friendly game of soccer and asked if he could join them. Grace and Sophie were immediately smitten by Zim's carefree air and charming smile. Noah, however, yawned and looked disinterested, while Jake eyed Zim up and down and said, "OK. Let's see what you've got."

By the end of the game, everyone was eager to make Zim their new best friend. He was a wiz at soccer, loads of fun to be around, and good-looking to boot. As far as new kids go, Zim was pretty darn cool. He'd won them over without really even trying.

The rest of the summer was a blur of activity. Zim was invited to join in on anything involving Jake, Noah, Grace, or Sophie. And Jake even asked him to join the William E. Zane, or WEZ, Knights soccer team! Official practice began in August, and by the time the first day of school rolled around, Zim had earned himself the title of "Zim the Soccer King," plus he'd made friends with all of the other members of the WEZ Knights.

So it was easy to look at Zim and assume he hadn't a care in the world—that the same world was his for the taking, and that everything came easily to him—but only if you were a surface looker. If you looked a little deeper, you could see that Zim, just like the rest of us, had doubts about himself.

For example, how could he be sure that Jake liked him because he was fun, and not just because he scored more goals than the other kids on the WEZ Knights? After all, Jake was the captain of the WEZ Knights and thought winning was just about the most important thing in the world. And how could he be sure that Sophie and Grace, who turned out to be the most popular girls in the class, liked him because he was a good listener and treated them with respect, the way his mother taught him, and not just because he was "cute"? After all, they were both really pretty, and it seemed to Zim that *pretty* pretty much always paired with *pretty*.

How could he be sure that Noah, who often came across as a little superior to everyone around him, liked him because he was funny and knew how to be a great friend, and not just because Sophie, Grace, and Jake all seemed to want him around? After all, being a part of the in-crowd seemed very important to Noah, and if Noah liked you, you were in.

Truthfully, being a part of the in-crowd hadn't seemed so very important to Zim—at least, not at first. He just wanted to have friends at his new school, and the in-crowd was the first group of kids his own age that he'd run into, and they had snatched him up quickly. It felt good to belong, and it didn't exactly feel *bad* to feel popular.

So when Maralissa Lou walked up to Zim during recess on the first day of school, Zim had a decision to make. And for the first time in his life, Zim's good heart let him down.

MARALISSA LOU

Maralissa Lou was undeniably different. For starters, what was up with that name? Most people felt sure his parents hadn't done him any favors when they saddled him with such an odd name.

But that's not how the Lous saw it.

Gwen and Donald Lou loved their son dearly from the very start. They had wanted a child for many years. When it became obvious that they were not able to conceive a baby on their own, they opted to adopt one. The "adoption option," as they fondly called the process, made them happy knowing that they could fulfill their desire to *be* parents by filling a child's need to *have* parents. When they found out they were to be parents of a small infant boy, they were absolutely thrilled!

And naturally, they wanted to give this baby boy a name of great significance—a name that represented all they hoped their son would be. A family name to show him that he was 100 percent and without hesitation a part of the Lou clan. So they created a name from the names of the two men they admired most in the world.

Gwen Lou's great-uncle, Mara McAmis, was a generous and loyal man. She loved him very much. When her own parents died suddenly in an automobile accident when Gwen was only five, Uncle Mara and Aunt Rhude took Gwen into their home and loved her as their own. So "Mara" seemed like the perfect name for a son, as far as Gwen Lou was concerned.

And Donald Lou's father, Alissa, whose name was Germanic in origin and meant noble and kind, was as noble and kind as the meaning of his name. Alissa Lou was a hardworking man who loved his family and donated much of his personal time to helping his community grow and prosper. He fought fires with the volunteer fire brigade and operated a soup kitchen on the weekends for those less fortunate. So "Alissa" seemed like the perfect name for a son, as far as Donald Lou was concerned.

Combined together they made Maralissa —a name that they proudly gave their son.

Had Zim been named Maralissa, the name would have been perceived as super cool. Zim could pull off any name with just a flash of his smile. After all, how many people do you know who are named Zim? The odds are not very many at all. But no one ever criticized *Zim's* parents for giving him such a name. Why? Because Zim made "Zim" awesome.

Maralissa, on the other hand, had to work extremely hard at wearing "Maralissa." Although he was every bit as generous, loyal, noble, and kind as his parents wished he would be, you had to be willing to look deep in order to see it. Sadly, it takes some effort to see below the surface. So because it is much easier, people often settle for being surface lookers.

And this is what Maralissa's surface looked like:

He had one too-small head with two too-large ears and a small crop of unruly brown hair right in the center of the top. All of this, teamed with a smattering of splotchy-red birthmarks that made him look polka-dotted and caused too much distraction to make noticeable the twinkle in Maralissa's small brown eyes or the warm smile on his face. And this out-of-the-ordinary noggin perched atop a scrawny body that had never scored a soccer goal because no one would ever dream of letting him play on their team.

Add to this the fact that Maralissa refused to have society dictate his sense of style. He preferred to create his "own look," which often left people uncomfortable since society generally believes that style is something you should *follow* instead of *create*.

Maralissa's current style was golf knickers with striped suspenders and brightly colored collared shirts. He preferred knee-high argyle socks with red boat shoes and a sideways baseball cap, worn only when outdoors. His favorite hat *du jour* was a bright red cap with "Big Guy" appliquéd in royal blue letters above the bill.

You might conclude that Maralissa just wanted to be noticed, if only for his clothes. Or perhaps he just *liked* his look. Either way, he was unique. So between the looks he had no control over and the ones that he did, you had to be prepared to encounter such a blaring volume of exterior.

And Zim was not prepared.

Zim was in the middle of telling Jake, Noah, Sophie, and Grace a really funny joke about a parrot and a plumber when

Maralissa edged his shoulder in between Sophie and Noah. Then, nudging his way in until he was directly in front of Zim, he looked around and said, "Hey, guys! This won't take a second and then you can get back to your joke. Or maybe you can start it from the beginning so I can hear too." Then directly to Zim he said, "Hi, Zim. My name is Maralissa Lou, and I want to welcome you to William E. Zane Elementary. I hope we can be friends and maybe talk for a while."

Zim had noticed Maralissa earlier in the day. Maralissa sat at a desk in the front of the room where it was easier for him to see the chalkboard. He was also a little hard to miss. But Zim did not expect the helpless and unnerving feeling of being faced with

Maralissa up close and personal. Zim could feel himself fumbling in his head for the correct response when Grace and Sophie began to giggle and Jake and Noah ran off calling, "Come on, WEZ Knights! Let's go play ball!"

Maralissa shrugged and smiled at Zim with sad eyes. He said, "I get it. I know my ears are kind of big and my hair's a wee bit strange, but that's the way that I was made. I don't think that I can change. Can't we be friends anyway?"

Zim felt a flush of shame for wanting to run from Maralissa. His heart was telling him, "This guy is obviously really nice, and he can't help how he looks. And so what if he dresses a little loudly?" Then Zim reasoned that hadn't he, himself, walked right up to this same group of kids not so long ago and invited himself in? But Jake and Noah were calling, and Sophie and Grace clearly disapproved of befriending someone so unlike themselves. So Zim ignored his heart, lowered his head, and walked away.

Maralissa called after him, "Hey! Why won't you play with me?"

But Zim just kept walking.

He joined the Knights in a game of soccer. And even though the team hoisted him on their shoulders and called him Zim the Soccer King after he scored the winning goal, Zim felt empty inside.

MISS PRUDENCE POPPYCOCK

This was to be Miss Prudence Poppycock's twenty-third year of teaching fifth grade at William E. Zane Elementary School. She was known throughout the school district as "No Poppycock," a nickname she'd earned with her *no-tolerance-of-nonsense* policy in her classroom.

Her first year as a teacher, fresh out of college and not looking or feeling very much older than the students she had been given the awesome responsibility of helping to shape and mold into forward-thinking and well-educated human beings, she had been faced with a dilemma. On the first day of school, she wore her favorite pleated skirt and a soft pink cashmere sweater—the one she thought most complimented her long, slender frame. She wore her soft brown hair in a loose ponytail and added just a touch of pale pink blush and lip gloss to her naturally pretty and sunny face. She wanted to make the best impression possible. Much to her dismay, many of her students mistook her for an older high school student sent into the classroom to assist the new teacher as an aid. Try as she might, she could not convince them that she was the new teacher and therefore they must do as she instructed. It was a disaster that Miss Poppycock had no intention of perpetuating.

So that night at home, after a dinner of homemade vegetable beef soup and a tall glass of cold milk, her go-to comfort foods, she devised a plan.

The next day, she entered her classroom with her hair pulled back in a tight schoolmarm bun and wearing stockings, sensible shoes, and a blue, ankle-length jumper over a blue- and yellow-striped sweater. The finishing touch: a pair of non-prescription, cat-eye glasses. She set her mouth in a firmly serious non-smile and spoke in a quiet, low, and no-nonsense manner. Thus No Poppycock and her *no-tolerance-of-nonsense* policy were born, and the children had absolutely no trouble believing that she was indeed the person in charge of her classroom.

Miss Poppycock firmly believed that "no" was the most loving word in the English language. She never threw this word around willy-nilly or used it out of spite. Instead she was careful to use it *only* when she really meant it and *only* when she was sure it was in the best interest of her students. After all, you have to love and care an awful lot about someone to tell them no when they would rather hear yes.

Miss Poppycock's teaching rule of thumb was to never smile at the students during the first month of school. This task she found particularly challenging, as she was so often amused by the humor and antics of her young charges. But her experience gleaned from that first year at William E. Zane had been that when she seemed extremely serious from the beginning, it was easier to enforce her *no-tolerance-of-nonsense* policy. After the policy was firmly established, she could loosen up a little bit, smile, and even laugh some because the students by then knew better than to be disrespectful.

Even though the students laughed and teased about stern No Poppycock, year after year she was voted their favorite teacher. Perhaps it was because the children always knew where they stood with Miss Poppycock, or because she loved them enough to say no to protect them when yes wasn't in their best interests, or because they knew they could always count on her for help. For whatever reasons, Miss Poppycock was loved. Even after Miss Poppycock met and married the man of her dreams, "JT"—a nickname that stood for "John Trackstar," which he earned during his athletic school years—and took his last name to become Mrs. Truman, and even after that when they began a family of their own, at school she remained Miss Poppycock.

Miss Poppycock looked forward to meeting her new class every year. She especially loved the joy with abandon that children express so well; the joy that is seen most vividly in the twinkle of their eyes. Yet Miss Poppycock had noticed a dulling of the twinkle in recent years. It seemed that youthful joy was becoming harder and harder to come by.

Why, just this morning, she had witnessed a brilliant twinkle in the eyes of Zim, a new boy at school. And the soft sparkle in the small brown eyes of a very special boy, Maralissa Lou, had warmed her soul. She had known Maralissa for his entire time at William E. Zane Elementary and had always marveled at his stubborn determination to keep his spark, no matter what.

She had experienced great hope for a rebirth of the twinkle in her classroom. But by the end of the day, the happy light of eager anticipation had disappeared from Zim and Maralissa's eyes. And just as she'd known that first day of school so many years ago, this was a disaster that she had no intention of perpetuating. Something must be done.

That afternoon on the way home from school, Miss Poppycock bought cold milk and the makings for homemade vegetable beef soup.

THE SECRET DRAWER

*D*ays turned into weeks and weeks to months, but nothing seemed to change. Miss Poppycock liked her students very much. They were obedient and respectful, but there was just a lack of spark. And there was always the question of how to help Maralissa fit in.

Maralissa kept his smile on his face. He continued to invite people to talk to him, or include him in play, with little success. If he felt sad, which surely he did, he tried very hard not to show it. He bravely treated every day as a new opportunity.

On the outside, Zim seemed happy and well-adjusted to his new school. He certainly had friends, he was making good grades, and he was still Zim the Soccer King, but something was missing on the inside. He couldn't shake the knowledge that he was not only letting Maralissa down by ignoring him, but he was letting himself and his good heart down as well. "How could I be so mean?" was the thought that continually gnawed away at Zim's consciousness.

During class time, Miss Poppycock certainly saw to it that no one made fun of Maralissa. And when it was time to work in groups, if Zim and Maralissa were paired together, they worked dutifully side by side. But during lunch and at recess, or in any activities independent of school, Maralissa was definitely an outsider.

Then, one day in early spring, Zim made a discovery.

Miss Poppycock had laid down the law. She was tired of messy desks, so she instructed everyone to empty them out and throw away the trash, and afterwards return their books, pencils, and notebooks neatly back inside.

Zim had finished throwing out scraps of paper, broken pencils, and eraser stubs. He then took the time to file tests, homework assignments, and reports into their proper folders and replaced borrowed books back on the classroom shelves where they belonged. He was really feeling good about restoring order to his surroundings. Just when he was about to return everything back into his desk, he spotted something he hadn't noticed before.

There, at the back of his desk's storage space, was a very small knob. When he pulled on the knob, out slid a thin little drawer just big enough for the miniature notebook nestled inside.

How could he have missed this?

Zim took the notebook out of the secret drawer to admire the hand-stitched cover that looked to be made of some lizard-skin-like material, with the coolest image of a dragon breathing red-hot fire stamped in the center.

"Whoa!" thought Zim. "If this was mine, I'd never leave it behind!"

Studying it carefully for the name of the owner, he turned it over and saw there, taped on the backside, a tiny white envelope with just one word written on the outside: "Zim."

Zim! This notebook was meant for *him*!

Zim glanced around the room to make sure no one was looking. He wanted to keep this discovery to himself, at least for the time being. Assuring himself that everyone was caught up in their own desk-cleaning projects, he carefully removed the envelope, slid his index finger under the flap, and loosened the seal.

KNIGHTS IN THE ORDER OF THE SECRET DRAWER

Zim cautiously removed the note from inside the envelope, unfolded it, and laid it flat on a page of an open folder where he could quickly hide it if anyone came snooping by.

It read:

Zim,

You have been carefully selected to serve as a Knight in the Order of the Secret Drawer. You are obviously clever and observant because you discovered the secret drawer all on your own. You will need these qualities to be an effective knight. It is an honor to serve as a knight, but service comes with great responsibility.

By opening your notebook and learning your quest, you agree to the responsibilities of knighthood. There is no turning back.

Are you up to the task?

Zim felt a strange mixture of uncertainty and excitement churning inside. Was he up to knighthood? This was certainly an adventure of the most extraordinary kind! Someone thought he was *knight-worthy*! I mean, of course he was already a WEZ Knight, but this was different. That was just the name of the fifth-grade soccer team. This was about being a *real knight*!

"The great Sir Zim! Honorable knight in the Order of the Secret Drawer!" Zim thought. His eyes began to gleam as he opened his notebook.

THE ZIM

Congratulations, Sir Zim!

You have just taken your first step toward greatness! As you surely already know, the sole purpose of a knight is to accept his quest and then set out to fulfill it.

Your quest is one of great importance. It will take hard work, absolute dedication, and determination to achieve your goal. But with confidence, you will succeed.

So first, you must find your confidence. You must recognize any self-doubts you may have and work your way through them. Your confidence is already there inside of you. Access it. Stand up straight and tall like the knight that you are. Think highly of yourself because you are good, fun, thoughtful, talented, funny, and uniquely you.

In order for you to begin your quest, you must first think very hard about what you like the most about yourself and why. Please write your answer down in this notebook and return it to the Secret Drawer.

Check the drawer tomorrow. Your quest will be waiting for you.

Could this really be happening? This was the most amazing experience ever! Zim found himself sitting up very straight. He actually felt knightly! He sat quietly and poured all of his thoughts into the best possible answer to the question, "What do you like the most about yourself and why?" and then he just knew. Hurriedly, he scratched his answer into the notebook, returned it to the hidden drawer, replaced all of his schoolbooks and supplies to his desk, and raced out to recess. He felt it in his bones: this was going to be *good!*

Zim couldn't wait to get to school the next day to see if he had really been assigned his quest. Glancing around the room to make sure no one was watching, Zim swiftly opened up the secret drawer and retrieved the notebook. *Yes!* His quest was waiting there for him!

Zim! I am so pleased to hear that your smile is your favorite thing about you. It's mine too! As a matter of fact, from the moment I first laid eyes on you, I nicknamed your smile "The Zim."

And you are right! Your smile does make people happy. And that is why your quest is to **find the twinkle!**

Part of your quest to "find the twinkle" will be to figure out what the twinkle is. HINT: Using your smile to make others happy will help you find it.

Go out, Sir Zim, and serve!

"That's it?" Zim thought, "All I have to do is smile? What kind of a lame quest is this? *Find the twinkle*?"

Zim felt a huge moment of letdown. For one big, fat second he was totally bummed. "Knights slay dragons and rescue damsels in distress! They don't *'find the twinkle'!*" he mused.

Then he noticed Maralissa Lou peeking at him from behind a ginormous world atlas that looked to be about twice his size and couldn't help himself. He smiled at Maralissa for the first time since the first day of school when he'd walked away from Maralissa's offer of friendship, and something in Maralissa's eyes changed. A kind of happy, hopeful gleam seemed to replace the dull, almost sad look that had been there since that first day.

"The twinkle," thought Zim. And it made him feel good. He had found it with his smile—just as the hint in his quest said he would! "Maybe being Sir Zim won't be so bad," he realized. So Sir Zim hopped up out of his chair and *Zimmed* everyone he came in contact with: his classmates, Miss

Poppycock, his mom and dad, and even the grouchy doorman who stood watch at The Celestial Pearl and never let Zim inside to visit his dad at work without growling, "Hey, kid, mind your manners while you're here." The twinkle began popping up everywhere!

Sir Zim kept at his task for several days. Every morning he found a new note in the Secret Drawer that made him feel good about his quest. Until one day he received this:

Sir Zim,

You are truly valiant in your use of The Zim. I commend you for the progress you have made.

However—

"However?" thought Zim. "This can't be good."

However, right now you are only a good knight. You have it in you to be a **great knight!**

You have accessed only one of your strengths: The Zim. Now it is required of you to do more.

Great knights lead by example. I think you know what I mean.

Zim's cheeks burned hot with … what was it? Anger? Frustration? Embarrassment? All three? Because Zim *did* know what was meant. It wasn't enough to just smile. And he also knew the implied "who."

If Zim was to be a great knight, he was going to have to face the damage he'd caused to Maralissa and his own good heart on the first day of school. This could mean the end of popularity. And Zim *liked* being popular!

But in Zim's head he heard:

First, you must find your confidence . . .

You have it in you to be a great knight . . .

Great knights lead by example . . .

By opening your notebook and learning your quest, you agree to the responsibilities of knighthood . . .

There is no turning back . . .

Are you up to the task?

Did Zim want to turn back? That would make him no knight at all! Worse than that, even.

Zim now knew what he had to do, and what his true quest was.

THE QUEST

At lunch, Sir Zim began his true quest. His hands were sweaty and his stomach was a little nervous. "But," he told himself, "I am a great knight, and great knights have courage!"

He walked right past the table in the cafeteria—the one where he sat every single day with Sophie, Noah, Jake, and Grace—*the* table that everyone wished they could sit at, where he, Zim, actually did sit. He found himself instead standing in front of a table in the far corner where, every single day, one person sat alone. He could feel a hundred eyes burning holes in his back.

"There's no turning back!" he breathed into every fiber of his being.

"Hi, Maralissa," Zim began.

Maralissa stopped mid bite of his bologna, cheese, and mustard on raisin-bread sandwich, a concoction of his own making that was just as unique as him, and waited for the rest without so much as a twitch of a muscle.

"I was wondering if I could take you up on that offer to be friends and maybe talk for a while. Mind if I sit here?"

Maralissa's grin reached from one too-large ear to the other as he said, "I heard you tell your joke about the parrot and the plumber. It was hysterical! Have you heard the one about the two baby skunks named In and Out? Would you like half of my sandwich?"

Zim sat down with Maralissa while Maralissa talked to him as if they'd been friends for their entire lives. And even though he was pretty sure he was making an epic social belly flop, Zim found he was wrapped up in Maralissa's conversation. This guy was *funny*! And Zim was 100 percent confident that Maralissa liked him for all of the right reasons.

THE TWINKLE

The next day, Aubrey and Caleb joined Maralissa and Zim at the table in the corner. The day after that, Mia, Michael, and Henry asked if they could eat there too. And then Kyle and Wyatt and Oliver and Zoe all asked. By the end of the week, people were pulling extra chairs up to the table and joining in on the fun.

Maralissa Lou had spent so much time observing everyone around him that he'd become a master impressionist. He could imitate ways of walking, accents, and facial expressions, and the kids found themselves rocking with laughter and begging him, "Maralissa! Do me next! Do me!"

At one point, No Poppycock had to come over and tell everyone to pipe down or she'd separate them all. But when her back was turned to them and she made her way back to the teacher's table, the twinkle in her own eyes burned so bright it could have illuminated even the darkest of nights.

Other knightly things were happening too. Not only did Sophie, Grace, Noah, and Jake leave *the* table to join the rest of the happy lunch crowd, but Sophie and Grace—who were exceptional at jumping rope—offered to teach Mia, Aubrey, and Zoe how to double Dutch while chanting, *"Ice cream, soda pop, cherries on top, how many boyfriends have you got? Is it one, two, three? . . ."*

And Noah decided to admit to himself that just maybe he wasn't the best at absolutely everything, and maybe that was OK. So he took Miss Poppycock's advice and asked Wyatt, the smartest boy in the class, if he would help him with math. Not only did Noah ace his next math test, but he found out that Wyatt liked building model airplanes too. They were going to go to Wild Bill's Hobby Shop together on Friday after school to choose a cool tri-plane kit to assemble while eating pepperoni pizza and watching old episodes of *The Three Stooges*, which they both *loved*!

It seemed everyone was in on the quest. The twinkle was back in full force, and no one, not even Miss Poppycock, who had twenty-three years to choose from, could remember a happier year at school.

A KNIGHT'S CONFLICT

The last day of school was fast approaching. Everyone was looking forward to all of the fun activities planned to cap off a great year and usher in the summer. No one loved the last day of school more than Jake because that was the day the championship soccer game was played.

This year, the WEZ Knights were playing the Franklin Force. It promised to be a tight match, so the Knights needed to be in top form. Jake *really* wanted to win that game and carry home the fifth-grade trophy. But he had learned a lot from Sir Zim's example and was dealing with a huge inner conflict of his own.

As team captain, he was in charge. He was responsible for everything! His team was made up of Noah, Sophie, Grace, Michael, Mia, Caleb, Henry, Aubrey, Kyle, Wyatt, Zoe, Oliver, and—best of all—Zim the Soccer King. In short, everyone in the class, except Maralissa Lou.

By now, the entire class had befriended Maralissa. They'd finally managed to get past his surface and down to the nice, funny, and thoughtful friend inside. Everyone, even Jake, really liked Maralissa, so Jake began to feel bad heading off to play soccer day after day—and day after day seeing the disappointed look in Maralissa's eyes.

On the one hand, he needed to do the fair thing for the team. How could he expect a win for the Knights with a kid as small as Maralissa in the lineup? On the other hand, he needed to do the fair thing for Miss Poppycock's class, and that included Maralissa.

Choosing between the two seemed *un*-fair to Jake.

WINNING

The day before the big game, as the Knights headed to the field for their final practice, Maralissa called after them, "Hey, guys! I hope you win! I'll be cheering for you!"

And Jake found his answer.

He just couldn't take the awful feeling of leaving Maralissa out for one second longer and heard himself yelling, "Hey, Maralissa! Grab a jersey and join us!"

The entire team began to cheer. "Hip, hip, hooray! Come on, Maralissa!"

When the whistle sounded the beginning of the match between the WEZ Knights and the Franklin Force the following day, the Knights came out raring to go. They were ecstatic with Jake's decision to invite Maralissa to play on the team—and that happiness gave them just the edge they needed over the Franklin Force. Zim immediately scored two goals, giving them a good, sound lead from the start.

But as they neared the end of the first half and Jake had yet to put Maralissa in to play, team morale began to fade. They left the field ahead two to zero but with much less enthusiasm than when they'd begun.

Grace was the first to speak up. "Jake, come on. Maralissa needs a turn to play."

"Look, Grace, I'm just as happy as you are to have Maralissa on the team, but I can't put him in until we are up by at least three goals," said Jake.

Maralissa nodded slowly, as if to say he understood, and said, "Thanks, Grace, but it's really OK. It's true: I'm pretty small. And I know winning is important to you all. The decision needs to be Jake's."

Jake rallied the team together for the halftime pep talk but without much success. A decidedly pep-less team headed back for the second half of play. The Franklin Force, however, was back in the game and ready to turn the score around. They quickly overtook the field and tied the game up at two to two.

Jake couldn't believe this was happening! No one—not even Zim the Soccer King— had their head in the game! Frustrated, Jake yelled, "Come on! Are we or aren't we the Knights?"

"Time out!" called Wyatt. "I need a team huddle!"

"What are you doing?" screamed Jake, "I'm the captain!"

"Yes, but I need for you to answer your own question," said a determined Wyatt. "Are we or aren't we the Knights?"

The whole team seemed confused, but no one more so than Jake, so Wyatt ran to the sideline, grabbed Jake's playbook, and ran back to the huddle. He opened the playbook, and inside was a miniature notebook with a hand-stitched cover made of lizard-skin-like material with a fire-breathing dragon stamped in the center.

The team let out a collective gasp.

"Well?" asked Wyatt, "Are—we—or—aren't—we—the *Knights?*"

"Where did you get that?" asked Zim.

"It's mine!" replied Jake. "I found it in a secret drawer in my desk."

The team gaped disbelievingly at Jake, until one by one it began to dawn on them what was happening.

"I thought I was the only one," said Zim, with a huge grin spreading across his face.

"So did I," cried Noah, Sophie, Grace, Michael, Mia, Caleb, Henry, Aubrey, Kyle, Zoe, and Oliver.

"Wyatt, how did you know?" asked Zim.

"It's because you're smart!" said Noah.

"Nah," said Wyatt, blushing a little. "It's not so much about being smart as it is about paying attention."

"Wait!" cried Jake, mentally catching up with the others. "Are we all *secret knights?*"

Bursting into laughter, the team answered as one, "YES!"

"Come on, Jake, a winner like you knows what to do," said Zim.

Nodding, Jake turned to the sideline and called, "Hey! Maralissa! Hustle up! I need you to come in for me!"

And would you believe it? It turns out Maralissa was not so much scrawny as he was wiry and scrappy. He was quick and sure-footed as well. A natural!

He ran out onto the field and zipped in and out of the Franklin Force, passing the ball back and forth with Zim until he, Maralissa, scored the *winning goal*!

Jake's mouth opened so wide in surprise that you could have parked a bulldozer in it. He, Zim, and the rest of the team could not have been happier to hoist Maralissa up on their shoulders and shout, "Hooray for Maralissa! The *new* soccer king!"

EPILOGUE

After the big game and the end of the year awards ceremony, Miss Poppycock hugged each of her students good-bye, bid them a fun and safe summer, and invited them to come visit her in her classroom next year.

And how pleased she was to see miniature notebooks covered in lizard-skin-like material peeking out of the backpacks and poking out of the pockets of her departing class. Her band of great knights had not let her down. The year of the Secret Drawer Club was a winning year indeed.

ABOUT THE AUTHOR

Barbe Turner

Eddie Coker

Barbe Turner graduated from Southern Methodist University with a BA in English literature and an elementary (K–8) teacher's certification. Funnily enough, however, her teaching experience embraces both ends surrounding K–8. She taught both a pre-school class with four-year-olds and a high school class called "Learning in the Community," before becoming a stay-at-home mother of three. Her children are now grown, and she is the grandmother of three. She is currently an operating partner in a company founded by her partner, children's performer Eddie Coker, and herself. Their company, okWard, is dedicated to educating both children and adults alike that it is not only OK but normal to feel awkward, and that we are all moving in the direction of being OK with who we are. Barbe lives in Dallas, Texas, with her husband and their three dogs. This is her first book.